Published by
Princeton Architectural Press
202 Warren Street, Hudson, NY 12534
Visit our website at www.papress.com

First published in France under the title: Attends Miyuki

Printed in China
22 21 20 19 4 3 2 1 First edition

This book was illustrated using watercolors and colored pencils.

Editors: Amy Novesky and Kristen Hewitt
Typesetting: Paul Wagner

Special thanks to: Paula Baver, Janet Behning, Abby Bussel, Jan Cigliano Hartman, Susan Hershberg, Stephanie Holstein, Lia Hunt, Valerie Kamen, Cooper Lippert, Jennifer Lippert, Parker Menzimer, Sara McKay, Wes Seeley, Rob Shaeffer, Sara Stemen, Marisa Tesoro, and Joseph Weston of Princeton Architectural Press
—Kevin C. Lippert, publisher

Library of Congress
Cataloging-in-Publication Data
Names: Galliez, Roxane-Marie, author. | Ratanavanh, Seng Soun, 1974-illustrator.
Title: Patience, Miyuki / Roxane-Marie Galliez ; Seng Soun Ratanavanh.
Other titles: Attends Miyuki. English
Description: English edition. | Hudson, NY : Princeton Architectural Press, A McEvoy Group company, [2019] | Originally published in French: Paris : Martiniere Jeunesse, 2016 under the title, Attends Miyuki. | Summary: When Spring arrives, Miyuki rouses her grandfather to greet the flowers in their garden, then embarks on a journey seeking pure water to awaken the one flower still sleeping.
Identifiers: LCCN 2019001589 | ISBN 9781616898434 (hardcover : alk. paper)
Subjects: | CYAC: Spring—Fiction. | Patience—Fiction. | Gardens—Fiction. | Nature—Fiction. | Grandfathers—Fiction.
Classification: LCC PZ7.G1373 Pat 2019 | DDC [E]—dc23
LC record available at https://lccn.loc.gov/2019001589

TEXT BY
Roxane Marie Galliez

ILLUSTRATIONS BY
Seng Soun Ratanavanh

Patience, Miyuki

PRINCETON ARCHITECTURAL PRESS
NEW YORK

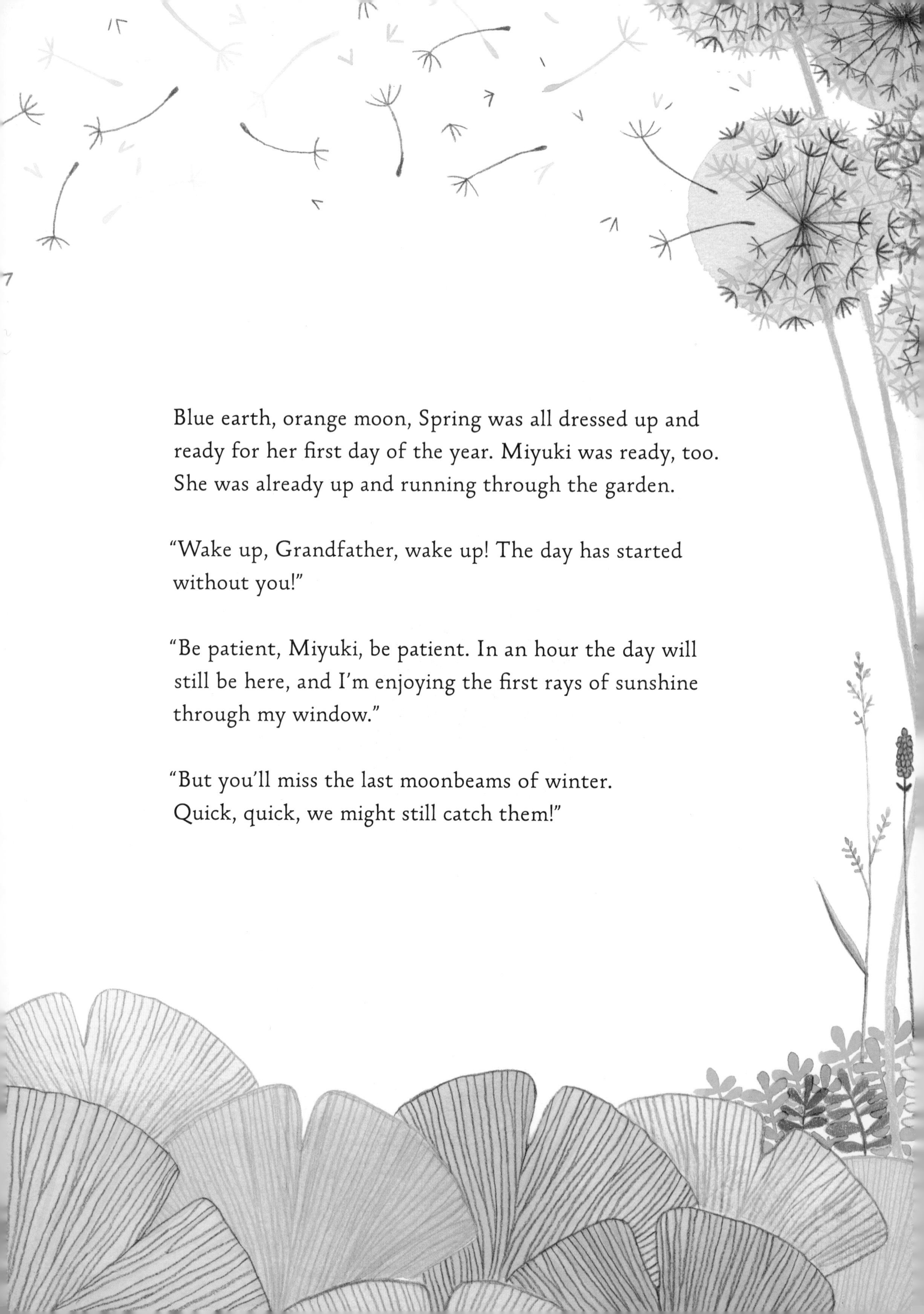

Blue earth, orange moon, Spring was all dressed up and ready for her first day of the year. Miyuki was ready, too. She was already up and running through the garden.

"Wake up, Grandfather, wake up! The day has started without you!"

"Be patient, Miyuki, be patient. In an hour the day will still be here, and I'm enjoying the first rays of sunshine through my window."

"But you'll miss the last moonbeams of winter. Quick, quick, we might still catch them!"

Miyuki hopped through the garden, and Grandfather trotted behind her. Together, they greeted each new blossom, and together they bowed to the wind.

"Good morning, cherry tree. Good morning, sweet grass. Good morning, flowers!"

Then Miyuki stopped at a little flower that was still asleep, unaware that springtime was beginning all around it.

"Wake up, little flower, wake up!"

"Be patient, Miyuki. This little flower is not ready to open. It is precious and delicate and needs the purest and finest water..."

Before Grandfather had finished speaking, Miyuki was already running to the well. The bucket banged all the way to the bottom. Instead of water, it brought back up a big toad.

"Quick quick, I need the purest water for my little flower!"

"Be patient, Miyuki," said the well. "It hasn't rained since the last full moon. In a few days, I will be full again."

Miyuki did not want to wait.

"Ask the clouds then. Maybe they can help you."

Miyuki ran, bucket in hand, to find the brightest and prettiest clouds in the sky.

But the clouds she found were too gray, too big, too far away. Then Miyuki spotted the perfect cloud.

"Pretty cloud, my little flower needs the purest water to wake up."

But the pretty cloud refused to give her its water.

Dismayed, Miyuki continued on her way and met more clouds.

Some offered her their water, but it was taking too long to fill her bucket, and Miyuki didn't want to wait.

It was already the middle of the afternoon, and the first day of spring was half gone. Miyuki kept walking, farther and farther from home, until she heard water rushing onto rocks and happened upon a beautiful waterfall.

"Waterfall, would you give me some of your purest water for my little flower?"

"My purest water lies in a lake, behind these falls. If you wait for night, when I am asleep, my water flows so softly you will be able to pass through to take some."

"Wait? I cannot wait, waterfall—I am in such a rush."

"If you cannot wait, then I cannot help."

Miyuki had been running all day, and her little bucket was still empty. A flower-filled house caught her eye. A young boy in a silver-moon-colored kimono was watering his garden.

"Could you give me some of your purest water? My little flower really needs it."

The boy wanted to know who Miyuki was and where she was from before he would agree to give her some of his water. So Miyuki told him her story. Then the boy filled Miyuki's bucket.

"Thank you!" Miyuki cried, and then she hurried home, quick quick.

Miyuki was running so fast she didn't see the stepping-stones on the path. Suddenly, she was falling. Miyuki's knees were scraped, the bucket broken, and the water all gone.

Evening was falling, she was far from home, and she was exhausted. Miyuki had been up since sunrise, trying to find the purest water for her little flower. And now the first day of Spring was almost over.

In that silent, still moment, Miyuki heard singing. She knew the song. It was the river that ran by her house.

"What are you doing so far from home at the hour when the moon outlines the mountains?"

"River, I'm lost, I'm tired, and I still don't have the purest water for my little flower. I don't have any water at all."

"Be patient, Miyuki. Sometimes it is necessary to slow down. I will take you home, and then you can have some of my water."

Lulled by the slow, quiet water, Miyuki fell asleep.

The river carried her home, where her Grandfather found her, picked her up, and put her to bed.

Blue earth, orange moon, Spring was all dressed up and ready for her second day of the year. Miyuki was ready, too. She was already up and running through the garden.

Grandfather was up, too, waiting for her next to the little flower. When Miyuki saw that the little flower was still closed, she started to cry. Two of the purest tears ran down her cheeks.

"Wake up, little flower, wake up."

"Be patient, my little girl. Neither flowers nor anyone in the world deserves to be watered by tears. Yesterday you ran away so fast, you missed the first day of spring. Come, sit close to me, watch, and wait for once."

Miyuki sat and watched and waited. She watched as Grandfather smelled the scent of a beautiful blooming flower with generous leaves. And she watched as, very slowly, he gently bent one of its leaves so that a few dewdrops, the purest water, slid down to the sleeping flower.

Then the little flower slowly opened.

"Good morning," the little flower said, "please forgive me for being late. I've been dreaming of Spring."